1980

S0-BOM-426

3 0301 00027325 6

LEAPING CLEAR

ALSO BY IRVING FELDMAN

LEAPING
CLEAR

AND OTHER POEMS BY

IRVING
FELDMAN

LIBRARY
College of St. Francis
JOLIET, ILL.

THE VIKING PRESS   NEW YORK

Copyright © Irving Feldman, 1973, 1974, 1975, 1976

All rights reserved

First published in 1976 by The Viking Press
625 Madison Avenue, New York, N. Y. 10022

Published simultaneously in Canada by
The Macmillan Company of Canada Limited

Library of Congress Cataloging in Publication Data
Feldman, Irving, 1928–
Leaping clear and other poems.
I. Title
PS3511.E23L4   811' .5'4   76-24914
ISBN 0-670-42182-0

Printed in the United States of America

Some of these poems previously appeared in *American Poetry Review*,
American Review, *Atlantic Monthly*, *The Bellevue Press*,
Boundary 2, *The Columbia Forum*, *Harper's Magazine*, *Michigan
Quarterly Review*, *The New Yorker*, *Poetry*, *The Yale Review*.

I wish to thank the Guggenheim Foundation for a fellowship grant
that enabled me to complete this work. —I. F.

811.5
F301L

University Book Service 28.7.78

90196

TO MY SON FERNANDO

CONTENTS

I

II

I

THE HANDBALL PLAYERS AT BRIGHTON BEACH

To David Ritz

And then the blue world daring onward
discovers them, the indigenes, aging,
oiled, and bronzing sons of immigrants,
the handball players of the new world
on Brooklyn's bright eroding shore
who yawp, who quarrel, who shove,
who shout themselves hoarse, don't
get out of the way, grab for odds,
hustle a handicap, all crust,
all bluster, all con and gusto all
on show, tumultuous, blaring,
grunting as they lunge. True,
their manners lack grandeur, and
yes, elsewhere under the sun legs
are less bowed, bellies are less
potted, pates less bald or blanched,
backs less burned, less hairy.
                                    So?
So what! the sun does not snub,
does not overlook them, shines,

and the fair day flares,
the blue universe booms and blooms,
the sea-space, the summer high, focuses
its great unclouded scope in ecstatic
perspection—and you see it too

at the edge of the crowd, edge of the sea,
between multitudes and immensity:
from gray cement ballcourts under
the borough's sycamores' golden boughs,
against the odds in pure speculation
Brighton's handball heroes leap up half
a step toward heaven in burgundy, blue,
or buttercup bathing trunks, in black
sneakers still stylish after forty years,
in pigskin gloves buckled at the wrist
to keep the ball alive, the sun up,
the eye open, the air ardent,
festive, clear, crowded with delight.

WAS

Was dark things bleeding away beyond
their outlines, was walls roaring, closing in,
or subsiding in bruised unaccountable
oblivions. Suddenly, the lights went on:
growing, he was learning, was learning that
bodies and things at ease in their auras
must not be touched until they consent,
can not touch until you say they can.

And everywhere the sun, the early light.
And they, with large features, with large limbs,
benevolent giants in bright colors
on the streets of Brooklyn, moving always
in relation, by courtesy and pleasure,
separate, with a glowing separation,
defined and with a glance of recognition
courting the other's sunlit advancing
definition, the other's passing wish.
Me first! deferred to *After you!*
—with a tip of the hat or a nod
or an arm waving one gallantly on.
There was nothing their enormous bodies,
their gentle manners had not simplified.
Here and there, around a subtle, a consen-

suous point, their purposes, their speeding
maneuvers and high heady murmurs met
and turned in a dance, a steady pacing:
their salutations smile, *Dear Sir Madam Child*!
their partings are signed with open gestures,
Sincerely Truly Cordially yours.
Distance itself consented, itself was touch.
A constellation swarming in the sun
in a common, a communing vibration.

And drifting at night, going to sleep,
he wished with what little of his will
was left, no longer to uphold
the gravity of everything. He said
they could, and saw them fall and flow
together, droplets with little lights
starlike, drinking one another mouth
to mouth, conjoining and clarified.
Under the roiling fluency, on the stones:
the body of transparence lying still.
Eyes open, lips to its boundlessness,
he saw this too, he saw it through and through.

WEASEL

Later, something else: sense
of secrets, choice, couplings, bias,
a broken consensus; sudden
nodes and surging, flares
over a field of crevasses.
Yearning incomplete tender
excited implicated in
the murder of communal majesty
reckless desperate pronged—he feel-
eeleels.
      Blackout.
And reappears: triumph
of skepticism in the guise of sex
—or the other way around—
a weasel in a wolfskin, appetite
probing forward, anguish biting back;
acrid awl-toothed ferrets, first
profaning mammal, his notions run
among the old identities,
grand immobile eggs of great saurians,
stave them in with a paw,
dabble sharp noses in the golden yolk
after the hidden copula, the payoff,
tit-for-tat, gobbet of muck on the palm.

What the hell is it all for?
run fast
consume and void
shake a paw at the shit.
Sudden turning, quick shying
of his snout in revulsion.
Despair composed this snob?
Airs blown
from distant bodies.
Digging down, flings dirt backward.
For great cravings small gravings.
And a muddy mouthful.
Screw my fellow man,
my putz is my brother!
Shame shunts him off.
Cross to the other side of the street.
Cover your tracks, move on.
Bestrides the ruined positions.
To live this caricature?
To *live* it.
Prong stiff into the March wind.

ISN'T

Except for reassembled curiosities,
inarticulate vast bone-stacks visited
by dank schoolchildren in dull museums
(half gawk, the others scrawl initials),
or thunder walking upstate in a low
rainless sky over miserable hamlets
where the dead cars brooding in dooryards
outnumber the starving inbred villagers,
scarcely anything survives from that epoch.

IS

Things as they are.
The even voice
weighs them together and says,
Such *and* such, on *both* hands,
see, clod here and *here* cloud,
as they happen to be,
their tactful balance.

The clod in the hand is heavy,
damp, dumb, grainy, old, cold, odd,
composite, shapeless, neutral, small,
sifted through the cleansing worm.
Well, so be it.
                    And so be it.
The sun comes over the cloud,
cloud comes over the clod
—the light, the light-of-hand—
and grass comes up,
singulars out of the earth
lifting their spears and shouting *Ahhhh*!

STANZAS: THE MASTER'S VOICE

Piddling small derivations with large
enthusiasm, taking his puddles for seas,
paddling in a sea of stimuli, to which
(such is play) he eagerly over-responded:
imagining perils and then the wave
that lifted him to safety while he struck
vainly at its steep and frightening flank,
then tumbled down bump on the waiting shore.
These were the pleasures of his setting out.

Of his arrival the pleasure was the sounds:
whistles, piping, voices, tall hooting in
the trees, among empty places, out
of high rocks uplifted like organ pipes,
clear calls in wells and holes and hollows and halls.
The world had voices, or was itself a voice,
a garrulous race that spoke without listening,
at random and loudly to no one he could see.

What did manners bid him do? Stay silent,
as one too young, as one not spoken to?
Or greet these breathings with his own replies?
He did them both, soundlessly opening his mouth
in tune and time to the calls that sang about,
that rang more faintly now with his grimacing.
And now beneath he heard the constant scratching sound,

like claws that scrabbled habitations in the stone.
That crackled in his ear as well—his own desire.
Silence then—and then a peeping repeated, like
a small occasional star, was all of sound grown pure.
To father voices, become my father! he swore.
Death had given him a master and vocation.

How easily his competence exceeds the song!
What the master could do once only and then
arduously, he achieves over and over
on the ample pages of his copybook.
He need not, does not, strive to compose. He writes.

The words enclose their own intention.
His art is writing, pure and simple.
He is the completed world's unfailing scribe.
What he writes repeatedly is simply perfection.

Diligence and stillness and peace, his lowered head
and pursed lips, are the little pastime of a large
distraction—he is listening to something else.

From the black shore behind the words, a small child,
a last master, is saying something he can't quite hear.

There is no time, this line has not been written.

BEETHOVEN'S BUST

To Richard Howard

The zero year, the dark eel body,
rushes forward, pours over itself
and disappears under the sky's black rock.
Suburban streets and rain in Buffalo
this Thursday night in harsh November.
City an instant above its falls.
The torrent smashes the lip and thunders
into a brief abyss; hither each guest,
trapped by his mediocre buoyancy,
floats on the swift affluence of conceit,
the sweet influence of wine and chatter,
of laughter, food, electric light.
And music now, a phonograph floods
the scene, a warming clatter of song
includes and moves whatever moves within
—and lends these particles a seemly
magnitude, these dissonants a structure;
so music rehears and rehearses, recalls
and recalls the irrevocable until
what cannot be revoked can almost be
desired, and the dumb fact is fate speaking.

In dry sufficient middle age
they come to on this nether shore,
gathered in bright rooms to toast
a *quartetto* on tour, four famous fiddlers

in turtlenecks and tuxes
who, beaming after Beethoven,
paddle the flux and artfully
snack up compliments like ducks.
Now Fortune wakes, now sits up
and rubs her eyes, presides
at the world's first levee.
These happy few, and if fewer
happier, are happy too to feel
their *angoisse provinciale* warming
to provincial self-complacence.
Glances are exchanged:
the continents and capitals
drift into range.
Passwords pass:
the universe is middle-class.
Whoever piqued themselves on making do
with second best, discover now they do not
know one another, have never met, maneuver
by delicate mutual repulsions,
veering to avoid the other's wake as if
it were a wine of desuetude that could make
them ponderous, bristling, and obsolete
—battleships among the swans.
                                    Indeed,
they strive to see beyond each other, vie
to see beyond each other's seeing, beyond
even the visiting stars, into
a place never seen, too transparent to be
a place, timeless, too bright. As far
as any eye can see all outside is
a belated guest running for the door,
then nothing more, the dark incivility,
the rain, more darkness, nothing more.
                                    Meanwhile,
the successes perfect their extraversion;
their glance when they look at others is bold

and gleams with pleasure and incredulity
—"What, you here? you lucky stiff!"

Whatever his luck, he too is here,
in from the rain to blunder for comfort,
the pleasure of standing in a crowd,
has brought his antique precocity,
his style the changeling prince—unknown
to himself and yet suspecting greatness—
his air startled, indignant, sniffish,
as if he'd caught the devil cheating at cards
or, simply, defecating on the deck.

Somebody's poet, he is introduced
to somebody's mother. It is poetry
they speak of, not motherhood,
though not at first, for first she recalls
her history, Junker girlhood, husband
—precocious martyr—murdered in a camp
in the 'thirties; then half casually,
almost a throwaway, "He was not even
a Jew. *Ach*, go read about it
in Shirer, if you like!" —gratuitous
infidelity from which she has not
recovered, will not, forty years after,
forgive.
          Recalling the irrevocable?
Well, music of a sort, someone gagging
on a spine. *This* horror doesn't go down
for all her swallowing, won't come up
for all her saying it out.
                         And has *he*,
he wonders, been accused, impertinent Jew
who did not die? He almost hears the slap,
death repeating its insult on her face,
sees the face stunned white with failure
before it stings red with shame.

So it is better to speak of poetry
—their theme, aptly, Death and the maiden—
while the dark eavesdropper, the final
husband, sidles closer with the shadows,
a mock-martini chilling in his hand.
Hair poked out like stuffing from a dollhead
tatter, face scored and delicate and white
—old shell or shipwrecked moon in daylight—
she calls for silence with yellowed fingers
and searching for words stoops and peers,
lady at the oven door who drags out
piping in their pie after fifty years
the verses of her German youth.

Hölderlin, Rilke, Mörike, Schiller . . .
the names of great dead poets drop.
Oh matinee idols of Eternity,
great brows and noses glimmering to
the farthest rows, the highest balcony,
their oversized Orphic heads now float
along the carpet's lotuses and sing
on death's Parnassus all the endless
artificial noon.
                    Just now, tonight,
they are praising loveliness of women
who know that poetry's a caress,
language purified to sweetnothingness,
showers of seed on a shadowy Eve.
Ruhe, Ruhe, she croons aloud. Remembrance
and reverie, release and rest,
engender in a vowel, *Ruhe, Ruhe*:
lulled, tumescent, gravid with
an endless, gray, and even sea,
its Baltic strand where, royal maiden,
she galloped brown horses in the foam.
And who can save her in the swart sea?
Follow me! follow me! the hooves plash away.

Poor bedeviled prince who cannot rest,
into the sea's little profundity
he whips his marvelous mount, out toward
the water charm, the voices, and the voice
within the voices, revealing his name.

Only the swell wrinkling under a wind,
a wake too wide to be a wake,
a world too wide to be the world,
nothing there, no one to save,
no maid, no martyr, no people,
and the prince himself gone far under,
weighed down by armor, waterlogged.
Only a child's kingdom under the wave,
the first light darkening, the faintest babble
from above, a muted sociable flutter
of tunings, teasing, footsteps, puffing
that blows out the candles on the cake,
a fading cheer! —music too awkward
and small, too homely and young to leave
its little orchestra, spoons shovels beds
(domestic murmur and tinkle and tears),
too brief to recall time from other places
or send it spiraling in long eddies.
A crone like a cork bobbing in time!
A generation whirled beyond his senses!
He braces to take it all on his back,
to uphold the flood, if flood is all there is.
Lungs scorched with salt, about to burst,
he sees the silver burble of his cry
gaily ascend the silent deep.
The chain of light fishes him out.

Surfaces and kicks for shore, escapes it all
—with what alacrity! Swallows sweet heavens.

So we are born, in our instant of greatest

terror. The mighty stay long until
they leap screaming for the world; others
patter in as lightly as the rain.
From nameless dying he could not bear,
he is born naming the horror, choking
on the name.
                    Dawn.
                              And now
you hear a first intelligent croak
sounding in the littoral grass
—human, almost; suddenly you
imagine the eyes, *if* you can bear it!—
then farther off and going fast, as though
toward its dismal lair, the patter perhaps
of light *faux pas*, then
a little sigh at last.

So, *voilà!* here they are after all,
high and dry in the corner
of a darkened parlor, on a sofa
tilting off toward the end of time,
mediocre muse, poor poet—he
doesn't please, she can't inspire—
cast away from the party together,
almost like maiden and boy
their matchmaking families marooned
and already seem hardly to miss
—while elsewhere in other rooms
the party sorts itself through chances
and changes, deferences and differences,
makes a sense of sorts circling around
its empty center, the dead one, the lost
martyr, the silence riddling the structure.

Let us step back now, as the lamplight
seems to, and permit them, semi-
strangers abashed and silent, to sit

forgotten where time's plunging
has flung them for a moment half-
unaware in puzzled abstraction.
Each, absorbed by his divergent dreaming,
dreams alone, but in our departing view
disposed as if they occurred
on a picture's visionary plane,
neutral, full, abstract, eternal
—she a princess at seventy
shaking off death's importunate arm
around her shoulder, he
a frog of forty
sitting on Beethoven's bust,
trying to understand.

LEAPING CLEAR

Circumambulate the city of a dreamy Sabbath afternoon. Go from Corlears Hook to Coenties Slip, and from thence, by Whitehall, northward. What do you see? —Posted like silent sentinels all around the town, stand thousands upon thousands of mortal men fixed in ocean reveries.   —HERMAN MELVILLE

1

Excrescence, excrement, earth
belched in buildings—the city
is the underworld in the world.
They wall space in or drag it down,
lock it underground in holes and subways,
fetid, blackened, choking.
                                  Shriveled, small,
grimed with coal and ash, shovel in hand,
his dust-sputting putz in the other,
like death's demiurge come up to look
around, to smudge the evening air,
the old Polack janitor on Clinton Street,
turd squat in the tenement anus,
stands half-underground in darkness
of the cellar steps and propositions
passing children in a broken tongue.
Quickly, they crowd, they age, they plunge
into holes, and are set to work.

2

Encountered at estuary
end across beaches and dunes,

or opening out of the breakwater's
armlock, a last magnitude
of bay, or beyond the crazywork
of masts and rigging down a street
suddenly, the sea stuns
moving into itself, gray over
green over gray, with salt smell
and harbor smells, tar, flotsam,
fish smell, froth, its sentient
immense transparent space.

Walking in Coney Island, bicycling
in Bay Ridge on the crumbling water-level
promenade under the Verrazano,
walking the heights above the Narrows, driving
on Brooklyn Heights, then slowly at night
under the East River Drive past the empty
fish market, past Battery Park, and then
northward driving along the rotting piers,
or looking downriver from Washington Heights
into the harbor's distant opening,
I recovered one summer in New York
the magical leisure of the lost sea-space.
Breathing, I entered, I became
the open doorway to the empty marvel,
the first Atlantis of light.

Windy sun below the Narrows,
Gravesend scud and whitecaps,
coal garbage gravel
scows bucking off Bensonhurst,
Richmond blueblurred
westward, and high
into the blue
supreme clarity,

it gleams aloft, alert
at the zenith
of leaping, speed
all blown to the wind
—what, standing in air,
what does it say
looking out out out?

And the light
                    (everywhere,
off ridge, rock, window, deep,
drop) says,
                    I leap clear.

3

Recalled from the labor of creation,
they were glancing as they flew, and saw
looking out to them the shimmering
of the million points of view. To see
Brooklyn so on a sabbath afternoon
from the heights, to be there beyond
the six days, the chronicle of labors,
to stand in the indestructible space,
encompass the world into whose center
you fly, and be the light looking!

The demiurge of an age of bronze
sees his handiwork and says it is good,
laying down his tools forever.
To see Brooklyn so in the spacious ease
of sabbath afternoon above the Narrows
is to say over and over what our speechless eyes
behold, that it is good, it is good, the first
Brooklyn of the senses, ardent and complete
as it was in the setting out of the sabbath.

II

After the fall of the republic, a panel of actors still in costume came on tv and told without hardly acting at all just how it felt being an actor. Their pluck and candor won them generous applause. Even the leaders of the claque were moved, proving that people are human after all.

LIBRARY
College of St. Francis
JOLIET, ILL.

90196

At the onset of an era of laughter, it was thought to restore the integrity of the temple with satire. How proficient everyone became (and how delighted to discover this universal talent)! Even the dullest were soon masters of ridicule and could satirize satire itself, while the few who could not grew expert in the modes of laughter. There was nothing but laughter—laughter and integrity.

When the blind dwarf (manacled, unkempt) was led in, the temple, as if not to be outdone, tittered and roared, cast itself down and rolled on the ground in a devastating parody of collapse. Nor were they spared who kept aloof—you, for example, who read this text smirking amid smithereens. Private smiles blend nicely enough into the general shambles of idiocy.

THE PRODIGAL

Fifty years and not a nickel to his name,
the fat lines of his credit expunged,
his heritage the milt-clouded muck,
he dreams he is a victim, dog-bitten,
flea-chancred—*The Disinherited One*
he calls himself, plunking down three last words.
And so he runs with the runts and weird,
the world's culls and thwarts, a desert wrath
slavering for the succulent towns.
His cohort, his conquering dolts, crowds
an outlying village street. *We have
come back!* they shout, but their joyous
mutilated cries summon no faces
to the horrified windows, bring salt
foaming out of the broken roadways.
Dire under the stars, they know it now:
earth detests them. They buzz about
in confusion, dismay, terror, rubbing
their snubnoses over long stupid cheeks
and turn their simple sullen faces
here and there, casting for a way back
into the wilderness—the founding fathers
of the second republic.

After the dioramas, the *Refugees Fleeing
on a Road*, the *Burn Ward*, the *Bomb Crater*,
and other such vivid scenes of war,
and live families of little Chinks
handing tea things 'round in a sewer pipe
—and oh as they stood there in awe at how
the lesser art of art could imitate
the greater art of war, that bulldozing,
those vivisections, oh stood naked almost
in awe before their awe, they felt that day,
one family among many, they felt
the force that surged along their linking hands
strike the dumb resistant wonder and slow
to a simple warm domestic glow,
they were happy to be there together—
and then the big blow-ups: world leaders
taking it easy at home, looking somehow
like family and sad like your old man
—all of it marketing the point about
war is h__ll in sharp, telling images—
well, when you pressed this certain button,
well, all of a sudden light and sound
started in, everything was all mixed up,
so confused you didn't know who you were
—it was like the world was going to blow!—
noise of armies clashing invaded

their ears, and terrible dark except,
behind red celluloid, rockets madly glared.
They crouched down and closed their eyes and were scared.

The light at the end of the tunnel proved
to be the orange roof of a restaurant,
a cockcrow of Early Colonial dawns.
There—under a mock-up of the Park,
oh it had everything, right down to crowds
of really tiny figures, themselves maybe,
each with a tinier dot of shadow like
a period lying painted at its feet,
it was, you would say, like heaven, seen
from far away, of course, and at the same time
you were in it—that was funny—and there
they sat down with other families
to portions of what turned out to be warm
shit.
    Well, then they knew the war was over
and which side won, which didn't much matter,
and bent their heads and said, Thank you, lords,
for taking reality out of our hands
and giving us the good life instead.

March 1974

Nervous and vital, he, too, danced forward to heave his flaming javelin at the band of elders who barred his way to the secret and the treasure. And yet, although he clamored and raged in the forefront, the attackers were so many, he found himself too far off to tell if he had dented that fussy reticence and dull certitude, that infuriating self-complacence. And if now and again one of them fell, it seemed, filtered through that distance, the result of invisible blows.

But when, long after, he had struggled to the top of the little eminence where they stood, his sword out to skewer the old bastards once and for all, they said, spreading their arms (and neither weakness nor fear could perturb their sluggish pentameters),

We thought you'd never reach us with relief,
you've been so long. Now come and stand where we
have stood, hold up the standard we've upheld!

Their standard (as he saw for the first time) of shame (as he thought almost for the last) was a bit of bloodied bedsheet, the elders feeble beyond belief, and their secret, their treasure, there below them on the plain, a city of graves. Now he understood they were in fact death's brightest, bravest face, turned not to guard but to hide—with overweening pity or else in shame they could offer no better—their horrid town from the eyes of the thronging young.

No longer a will and its blindness but a fatality and its intelligence (such as it was)— and no less embattled than he'd always been— he, too, with a senile passion for repetition, tirelessly joined in the carping antiphon, barking out his odious part at the horde pressing toward them,

Stay where you are!
                    So it has always been.
So must it always be.
                    I told you so.

To be innocent must be simple enough, but how is one to assent to justice?

Grinning their triumph in the local court, his lawyer shakes hands with himself on high, claps an arm around Robert's shoulder and waggles aloft two splayed fingers to the sparse crowd—while Robert morosely appeals the verdict. Better condemned (if need be) by the highest court than acquitted by any other.

Mere! ludicrous! overweening! vanity. Litigious! Ungenerous! Unjust! his lawyer taxes him in ascending scale. But Robert will not forego the bitter privilege of his grievance, or—dull culprit before, brilliant plaintiff now—renounce the little edge of indignation it has given him on the universe.

Let him raise tiny fists and bawling eyes to heaven, pummel the air, thunder aloud, no greater jurisdiction answers, no higher judgment is forthcoming. And Robert is condemned to the singular case of himself—his principle, his progeny—while all about him clients and lawyers huddle together, buzzing in the black offices of their ears.

Trying to think yourself backward out of is how you discover philosophy—in the trap. Naturally, you suppose blindly living forward got you into it, the trap. In this, like the fox—who gnaws his foot, having come to believe (reasonably, since its pain attacks him) his foot is the trap.

Things cannot be so simple for you. Backtracking, you fit your three into the four that first came your way. Always out of time, your escape from *this* trap is, over the long run, to devour yourself completely—and you are to be last inferred daintily stalking the day-spring on four phantom feet.

Once out, once free, you comprehend that as the air comprehends this. Life takes the bait, thought incorporates the trap.

ANTONIO, *BOTONES*

para Aguirre

Tourist, traveler, consider this child:
Antonio, *botones** of the Ida Hotel,
of every hierarchy the base,
the bottom of every heap. Oh too clearly
one sees it: vainly God flexes and waxes
His most apparent effulgence, wanly
He wanes in the lens of the soul of
Antonio the dull, the unperceiving.
And a little lower only, the Caudillo
(who dreams he is a boy pillaging apples)
has thrown an aged leg on the high hedge
of heaven and tottering atop the backs
of his Ministries (not excluding *Hacienda*,
not forgetting *Información y Turismo*)
tries to hoist himself up and clamber over.
Push, push, push me higher! his order flies
down from the apex of effort, along the chain
of command, by way of the Ida's owner,
its "mater dee," desk clerk, barman, straight down
to Antonio in the lobby. And there
the little bell is pinging wildly, Oh please,
Antonio, for the love of heaven, just
a tiny bit higher!
                                And he on whom so much
depends, his jacket spattered, one button

*Spanish: bellboy.

dangling, ears clotted with cotton, his eyes
glazing, his nose just about to be picked,
Antonio the absent-minded, the emptyheaded,
sleeps on his feet, hears nothing, fails to grab
this client's valise, to open the outer door,
or pick up an unspeakable butt
disgracing the lobby and the noble carpet
—and witless, unwitting, spares the Caudillo
ultimate vulgarity: success in heaven.

Lowest of the low, Antonio, *botones*
of the Ida Hotel (two stars twinkle
on its lintel), Antonio, lowlier still
than the hem of the little chambermaid's skirt:
he's like the earth and like the feet of turtles
—he bears all slowly, himself stays hidden.
The traffic flow of orders down the pure,
the crystalline pyramid terminates here
in a puddle, a cipher, a fourteen-year-old failure.
Others glimpse the summit, hear a faint cacophony,
the Leader's stertorous cries, and they respond,
they go higher, come closer, see clearer—but not he.
Then who will clean the lens of Antonio's soul,
so smutted and smutched, so foggy and gray?
Not the Caudillo and his ministers; not
the technocrats, their meager darlings; or
the middle-class poets of Mao who chant
the pompless despots of the magic capitals;
not the saints in their cells, or cadres in theirs.
True, each one wants Antonio for his army
(maybe he's a muse? he seems to inspire them all,
for his sake they pray, profess, or rule—they say)
—but something in this world has to be gray.
Then let it be the soul of Antonio,
unsalvageably so!
        See,
wipe the slate clean, the slate stays gray!

—and makes the more brilliant those brilliancies
that great men scrawl ... all over Antonio, who else?
... before they pass on (and, naturally, don't think
to tip). Never mind! humble beneath humility,
he asks for nothing—it makes the ages weep.
Never mind! so faint, so fine the line between
acceptance of everything and consent
to injustice, the saints, the very saints
in bliss, even San Anónimo in his,
eyes blinded with their souls' own radiance,
drag chains across it continuously.
Never mind!
—Shall shade shine, or earth be lustrous?
—Oh surely not until the fiery blast
of God's breath pronounces final judgment!
But brilliance justifies itself, you say, and I
agree, I agree to all this glory
                            —and yet,
tourist, traveler, set down your suitcase here awhile
(yes, let's get down to cases),
consider Antonio, how his father comes
and beats him, how he takes his money, how
the Caudillo, impaled on the hedge of heaven,
cries aloud in his agony, If only
this innocent would try a little harder!
and urges him on for the glory of Spain
and its rightful place in the Common Market
—useless, of course, but what can you do?—
and how his boss, fed up to here, throws him out
and two days later can't remember his name
—while prancing ably in his place you note
his junior *confrère*, the former incumbent of
the Suiza y Niza (one star) down the street.
Consider Antonio, this simpleton,
this put-upon unresentful child, who can't smell
the carrot (yet feels the stick), who elicits
your sympathy as he thwarts your interest,
who tempts you to tamper with injustice

—only to drop your luggage on your feet:
                                        cram
your pride of life in his lens, see the world
as he must see it—then your eyes are stiffed,
then spasm cramps your brains, then effulgence
stains and shining shames and brilliance blemishes.
—Oh impossible to live there, awful to visit!
Nothing to do but take off on a trip
—and leave Antonio, incorrigibly
unpathetic, unorganizable as dirt,
creatively screwing up still another job.

But who is this leaping for your valise?
Well, it's not the local clod, it's not
Antonio, thank God! What a relief! Someone
a centimeter taller, some blue-eyed go-getter,
leaps for the desk, leaps for the door, his buttons
blinking your warmest welcome, Francisco
by name. Now here's a boy who doesn't appall
the clientele or his bosses. Efficiency's
transparency, looking at is seeing through;
it's like the swallowing of a good gullet;
no glum opacity, no crap in your craw,
nothing retrograde: indeed, the future
personified beside a revolving door.
One sees beyond him to the world as one
has always wished to see it—sunny Mallorca!
under the international sun, white furnace
of a furious polyglot declaring
in simultaneous Swedish, English, French:
I too am a tourist rushing here and there,
although, truthfully, nothing new is under me,
a man of my time until I'm pensioned off
and relocated semi-permanently
—among damp shadows of the cheaper season
on a tideless island, with no tongue of my own.

August 1974

· 37 ·

THE SECRET WORK

Nadezhda Mandelstam has told the story. In Strunino, after her husband's arrest, working the night-shift in a textile factory, she runs, sleepless and distraught, among the machines, chanting his forbidden poems to herself to preserve them. And so for twenty-five years in Perm, in Moscow, in Voronezh, Leningrad, Ulyanovsk, Samatikha...

A man with chills hugs himself,
rejoicing in his fever. She,
the frozen century's daughter, rejoices
in her secret, hugs to herself
the prophet hiding in her breath,
the infant she keeps close, safe, swaddled,
speaking.
        She covers over, makes him
smaller, safer, no bigger than
a seed, a spark—search where they will,
they will not find him here, yet here
he is, a little voice praying,
an enormous voice prophesying,
this live coal held on her tongue
burning behind clenched teeth.

To herself, *in* herself, over
and over, what must not
be said aloud, not written down,
not whispered in corners or left
to be smelled out clotting
at the ends of broken phrases
... the poems of Mandelstam
going out in Siberia's night.

III

1

Not
this mind,
these puns, a periplus
around a cosmion,
not mind widening this egg
to whiteness, a
universal, an o-
void in an omega, mind's
timeless waste:
poor
farm
pure
form;
not its dance of staggers, lame
capering caliper tacking
pegleg to legleg,
a moving mutiny around
a mute unity

that curves from salience
to silence, minding the store
with round redounding, O
mumly peepless!
its white the neutralest

effulgence;
                    no, not
mind, blind in the blank,
feeling a way by longings,
shortcomings, listing at large
a topography of stumble,
ego type-tapping, *Eggo*
eggo echo eccomi!
replicating aspects of egg
as ectoplasm, a ghostly
difference,
                    while going
about egg's beaued belly, belled
back—O, mothering curve
of contemplation!—mind
muttering, mumming;
                    not
this oaf of I'lls and ills, pale
aleph, cipher, white blighter
on its dancing chip over the dark
deep: not this mind in terror
of time, bringing its white treasure
on the wild tangents, yawing farther
into itself, its lurid, its phantom
sea;
        not this, not
these.

2

O
-word, the
bird's cry, the o-
vum comes
in a cluck, in a clackle
of slime and lime:

this
egg
is
fresh,
minty and sage,
a wight right in greenward weeds
beside the green sea
at dawn,
this egg is all
for the day's throne,
the sun's slide up the sky.
Inside, a joke, a son
in a see, an I
in an eye in an *Ei*: these puns
are fatal are
fertile,
duplicating with a difference
a various redundancy,
the gold conflagrance
that differs into a dupling heart,
an oeufre,
orfèvre of or-feathers
-fingers -feeders -features -fecker!
An incubus.
An imp-unity.

Time crows over the crackling and over
the rising sun, The difference lives!
The chickling cheeps, I am the difference!

3

Madam, Sir, abashed and saddened before
your own, your particular fates
—to differ, double, die:
Smile, idiots, look
at the birdie!

FATHER AND SON

Set against each other, ready to butt
and struggle, with the same glaring look
of the eye and fiercely vivid anger,
son and father, isolated together
in daily deadlock, their form of murder.

Not sacrifice: murder. For it matters
that no command has brought together
the proud and loving father, the eager son,
mercurial and defiant, his image,
or ordered the day and brushwood for the fire.
This is no test, but plainly real,
this Moriah where, unsanctioned, unblessed,
unpunished, sons and fathers pause and wait,
and nothing is revealed.

Will no miraculous ram now come
bleating, trotting, wagging his head
like a slow wisdom on an antique page,
misleading death for the future's sake
and calling back the pair in pity
of the boy's innocence, the father's love?

No ram. None. Wildly, the father casts
about the rocky field, and grapples for
imagined horns to wrestle out a ram

from nothingness, as if to drag a god
into the stunned impenetrable world
and feel the rough material horn,
the rank fur, the uncomprehending staring eye,
and behind it the startled air's commotions
where invisible hooves are bracing—while,
almost glowering, the pitiless son looks on.

Piercing the frozen scene,
is it his own? or his son's?
or an ancient cry deafening his ear?—
the shriek this faithless toiling father hears
and one moment thinks a hesitant bleat
before he mingles death with his generations.

1

Girls he took from friends at seventeen
he lost in months and never found again.
Not so the books he stole that year:
face à face with his pounding heart
a *Fleurs du mal* translated to fact
under the null persona of his coat,
and closer still, like a blade slipped
through the dark intercostal spaces,
Eliot's *Poems* spirited from Macy's
in a folded X-ray of his lungs.

When he read "Prufrock" in the subway home
that afternoon, he was a cat crouched
before a saucer of milk: nothing moved
in all that train that illicit hour
but the pink tip of his tongue
and the white pages turning.

2

He waited all that year where three
roads meet—love, art, thievery—
in a wilderness of rumbling stone

while the great caravans went by
surging with goods and grief, waited
for lightning to point the way.
Lightning struck.
Was it defect of intelligence
or excessive timidity, a curse
that made vapid the family seed,
or simply an instant's inattention,
the tiniest mothhole bitten clear
through the universe? what made him mistake
words for the lightning that lit them,
bowls of milk for ah! bright breasts?

3
Oedipus or Sophocles:
The Road Not Taken

He has been telling it with a sigh
—for sure!—ages and ages since.
Who might have gone limping toward Thebes
came prattling to Athens.

1

Check-grabbing in the neon effluvium,
the big spenders hustle from the table.
"I'm fresh out of singles. I'll getcha
later, Joey," they yell the waiter,
or "Here, kid, keep the change."
The change the change the change divides
and redivides fermenting in the chamber
of the unbroken floatable twenty,
lifeboat tilting on a depth of measureless
green, where you and you and you
and the waiter yaw in the wake
of the 40-long with sharp lapels
that swaggerdashes out lifting an arm
that shows two inches of white-on-white,
a watchband glinting, a ring with red stone.

2

The bigshots bang down their phones
like guillotines. Buy Marvin!
Sell Harvey!
Headless Harvey!
Paraplegic Marvin!

Gas presses on the stomach.
God, let me belch Harvey, let me
evict Marvin!
The office girls hurry. "Mr. Sam,
Mr. Sam, you didn't take your pill
this morning. You'll *kill* yourself!"
He sighs. All over the world
the cigars go out again. And a good
man, among mother-daughter-
mistress-wife, reaches the end
of his bicarb.

Among the absolute graffiti which
—stenciled, stark, ambiguous—command
from empty walls and vacant lots,
POST NO BILLS, NO TRESPASSING HERE:
age and youth—Diogenes, say,
and Alexander, dog-philosophy
and half-divine, too-human imperium—
colliding, linger to exchange ideas
about proprietorship of the turf.
Hey, mister, you don't own the sidewalk!
Oh yeah?
Yeah! the *city* owns the sidewalk—*mister*!
Oh yeah! says *who*?
Thus power's rude *ad hominem* walks all over
the civil reasoner, the civic reason.

Everyone has something.
Everything is someone's.

The city is the realm of selves in rut
and delirium of ownership, is property,
objects made marvelous by prohibition
whereby mere things of earth become ideas,
thinkable beings in a thought-of world
possessed by men themselves possessed by gods.

So I understood at twelve and thirteen,
among the throngs of Manhattan,
that I dodged within a crowd of gods
on the streets of what might be heaven.
And streets, stores, stairs, squares, all
that glory of forbidden goods, pantheon
of properties open to the air,
gave poor boys lots to think about!
And then splendor of tall walkers
striding wide ways, aloof and thoughtful
in their nimbuses of occupation,
advancing with bright assurance as if
setting foot to say, *This is mine, I
am it*—and passing on to add,
now yield it to you, it is there.
Powers in self-possession, their thinking
themselves was a whirling as they went,
progressing beyond my vista to possess
unthought-of worlds, the wilderness.

These definitions, too, have meant to draw
a line around, to post and so prohibit,
and make our vacant lot a sacred ground.
Here then I civilize an empty page
with lines and letters, streets and citizens,
making its space a place of marvels now
seized and possessed in thought alone.
You *may* gaze in, you *must* walk around.
—Aha (you say), conceit stakes out its clay!
—*That* is a cynic's interpretation,
pulling the ground out from under my feet;
I fall, I fear, within your definition
which, rising and dusting off my knees,
civilly I here proclaim our real estate,
ours in common, the common ground
of self, a mud maddened to marvel
and mingle, generously, in generation.

A PLAYER'S NOTES

To Hashim Khan

1 There is impatience in many disguises—weariness, reluctance, zeal, the desire to win, the fear of losing.

2 What is not impatience is the game, pure and simple.

3 Properly presented, with patient attentiveness, the ball is a surprise his opponent would not wish to refuse, will, with appropriate care, wish to return in kind.

4 Failing to attend to his opponent, he is doomed to try to exceed himself, is doomed further to succeed in defeating himself.

5 Playing for self-transcendence, he wastes and destroys himself, lags behind in order to fly forward too fast at the last instant.

6 Always the phoenix, unhappy bird who appears only on the threshold of the calcined house.

7 The game is not intended to flourish on the wreckage of reality.

8 Truly, reluctance (weariness, failure to attend) causes him to arrive late for the ball. Just as truly, his desire to fly, his dream that he can fly, that he is flying, cause him to arrive late for the ball.

9 The daydream of flight spreads its phantom pinions in the lost instant of his failure to attend.

10 Dropped onto the treadmill of his daydream, one ball will never reach him, while the other in the freedom of the game rushes past with a savage whirring of wings.

11 Gasping for breath, he asks, Is it possible to survive here without being reborn?

12 Rebirth—if that is the issue—comes from renewed contact with the eternal, as in its momentary flight on the court.

Therefore, these are forbidden, these are enjoined.

13 Forbidden: hairsplitting, pessimism, fantasy.

14 Enjoined: knowledge, good humor, the exchanging of gifts.

From the first, the gods were strangers who came among them, observing but keeping their distance, not sitting around the fire exchanging morsels or anecdotes of the road, not mingling under the blankets or quite meeting their eyes in the morning.

Gradually, therefore, they sought to catch their eye, to be acknowledged, finally, at all costs, to seduce the gods. The violence of their gestures in the dance, of their shadows around the fire, of their copulations could not compel the interest of the gods who appeared to desire neither their triumphs nor their sacrifices, not their success in the hunt or their most fruitful delvings or the signs and objects by which they thought to assure these.

They came at last to ignore the gods, then to forget them, and went about their affairs as before, although now each thing seemed united with indifference, seemed to possess a neutrality, a final clarity that could have come, as they had already forgotten, only from the gods.

A LITTLE BOY SAID

To Fernando, who said it

"Every time we die," a little boy
said, "Every time we die, there's Greeks
fighting again"—at their little Troy,
I add, and being a clangorous clock's
skirmishing, do not destroy.

So, when the mind exhausts its day,
Greeks jump up with clashing joy,
fresh from centuries of play,
and light the mind of a little boy
forever and ever and a day.

And tonight, somewhere a fiery Troy
glorious on the cindered ground
wakens near a sighing boy—
eyes, teeth gleam; armed men, rewound
to fight the void with fire and marvelous noise,

deploy along the brightening ground ...
I envy him his philosophic toy.

When everyone was going out
to brilliant day, to vivid night,
something had to be given up,
years ago when the world began,
something had to be left behind:
a token to darkness
a prize to the past
a nod to night
a nickel to mortality at the gate.
Let it be me! they said,
me, me, *I'll* stay.
I sew the world asleep!
I hammer the world awake!

Who *were* they? you ask.
The tiniest old men
who never were born,
twins, in fact,
and bent together
like halves of an O
but back to back,
a thousand years they'd need
just to straighten up
—what stubbornness, such loyalty
to the shape of a room!
And such doom

—like two little children
trapped in old age,
who can't grow up, who can't grow back.
A nailer, a tailor,
the one and the other.

And here today, right now,
at the top of the stairs,
with bent-up nail
and beat-up chair
on a broken floor
with a hammer only
and all of his might,
the nailer hammers, he hums
aloud to himself,

"Hey, watch out,
stand back there,
don't crowd me!
Dummy, can't you see?
this hammer's no toy,
the thing itself!
a hammer for real,
wood handle, iron head,
just see it flash
its sky's-worth of arc,
it drives home
in a single blow!
—the whole of heaven
on the head of a nail.

"Now who would have thought
you could get so much
on the head of a nail?
A nail? a nail? who said a nail?
Children, did *I* say a nail?

Now you've gót my goat.
I don't *need* a nail.
See, I throw it out
and I hammer away."

True, true, he hammers away.

And back to his back,
his brother stoops,
too patient, too still
to stitch in time,
with one little needle
and one bit of thread
and one ray of light
where dust specks blaze,
where filaments float:

"Cloth is waiting,
the button waits.
I squeeze my eye
to needle's eye.
By smaller degrees
and more and more quietly
and last so you can't even see,
I bring the thread near."

Then they glow in the trap
and they answer each other:
I pound the world apart.
I sew the world to stay.
Here's a knap on your noodle.
Here's thread in your eye.
I speak louder.
But *I've* the last say.

Bang! says one.
Shhh, says the other.

IV

THE GOLDEN SCHLEMIEL

So there's a cabbie in Cairo named Deif.
So he found 5,000 bucks in the back seat.
So meanwhile his daughter was very sick.
So he needed the money for medicine bad.
So never mind.
So he looked for the fare and gave it back.
So then the kid died.
So they fired him for doing good deeds on company time.
So the President heard it on the radio.
So he gave him a locally built Fiat.
So I read it in the papers.
So you read it here.

A poor man has less than weight, has negative
        gravity, his life a slow explosion. Barely
        he makes the days meet. Like doors they
        burst open. Money, job, daughter fly a-
        way from him. Irony, injustice, bits of
        horror come close, cohere.

They are with us, the poor, like the inner life
        which is wantless too; our souls' white
        globes float somehow in the blue, levi-
        tating and bobbing gently at middle
        height over the bubbling fleshpots.

Our effort to remake the found world as the
        lost reverie is desire.

So, little Yasmin was sick, sick to the point of dying.
She was like a garden coughing and drying.
And suddenly her salvation was there, a sheepskin, yes,
a satchel of money meekly baaing from the rear.
A miracle in the offing?
That famous retired philanthropist named God
was back in business? was starting to take a hand?
directing things maybe from the back seat?
Maybe.

Restored to its rich owner (he tipped a fig
        and a fart, a raspberry of plump nil),
        lying safely on his lap, the money was
        mute again, was superfluity, and root and
        sum and symbol, both lettuce and lump,
        of all evil.
She too approaching that state,
Yasmin, a flower, meantime, dying.

For the locally assembled daughter a locally
        assembled Fiat.

Too wantless to imagine the money his?
Spurned the miracle and thwarted the grace?
So loved the law he gave it his only begotten daughter?
Effed and offed his own kid?
Saint and monster, poor man and fool,
slowly exploding, Deif all this.
Yes, one melts at his meekness,
scoffs at the folly, trembles
for his stupor of bliss of obedience,
gasps at his pride, weeps
for his wantlessness,
grunts when irony that twists the mouth jabs the gut.
Then horror—the dark miracle—roaring, leaps
into the front seat, grabs the wheel and runs you down in the
        street
—while you sit on a café terrace innocently reading the paper

or, bent above a radio, feel the news waves break against your
   teeth.

Deif in grief. Deif in mourning. Deif bereaved.
Deif in the driver's seat. Deif without a beef.

And daily in four editions and every hour on
the hour, the media heap your dish with images
of sorrows and suffering, cruelty, maiming, death.
(Our real griefs in their imaginary jargons.)
And you cannot touch a single sufferer, comfort
one victim, or stay any murderous hand.
Consumer of woes, the news confirms you
in guilt, your guilt becomes complicity,
your complicity paralysis, paralysis
your guilt; elsewhere always, your life becomes
an alibi, your best innocence a shrug,
your shrug an unacknowledged rage, your rage
is for reality, nothing less. Yes,
you feel, murder would be better than hanging around;
if only your fist could penetrate the print,
you too might enter the reality of news ....
You switch the radio on, hungrily turn the page
of sorrows and suffering, cruelty, maiming, death.

Pasha, President, playboy swing masterfully
above our heads—what style! what heroes!—fling themselves
over the headlines into the empyrean
beyond our lowly weather—ah, *there* all the news
is blue and blank, those soarings, those mock descents
are *them* writing their own tickets in heaven.
Fortune, true, is spiteful and fickle, and glamour
itself must stalk them—but cannot shoot so high
as impotence dreams, as resentment wishes.
Gorgeous, limber, and free, like our consciences,
a law unto themselves, a darker law to us
—in their suntans our shadow.

And where they fly, the lines of force accompany,
the patterns of deference continue to comfort,
a maggotism distracting irony.
Their rods flatten others, their staffs flatter *them*
—you and I pay for the lies we get,
but heroes get the lies they pay for.
So here's the President's ear on the radio's belly
—if there are rumbles in Egypt, he'll know it,
he'll proclaim, Fix this! (Fixed!), Do this! (Done!).
And here is Deif's story beating at his eardrum.
Tremble, mock, shrug, or writhe, you and I
cannot write the ending, cannot snatch glory
of authorship from the anonymity of events.
The President can. The President does.
His literature is lives, is Deif smiling:
golden, seraphic and sappy, sheepish, sweet;
is Deif not understanding a thing and grateful
and happy like a puppy given to a child.
He speaks: his fiat is a Fiat,
assembled locally and worth five grand
(out of the President's pocket? Pal, guess again!)
—which cancels Deif's deed down to the penny.
Deif has no claim on the moral law, no dignity,
no destiny, no daughter; his suffering
won't embarrass, his monstrousness appall;
injustice is removed, and nothing left in its place,
the spot swept clear, blood expunged, crowd dispersed,
and Deif himself sent to park around the corner,
a bystander to his life, a pure schlemiel.
Deif never did anything, nothing ever happened
—all for the greater glory of the State.

Exit Deif with his dead daugher in his arms.
Re-enter Deif in a Fiat meekly beeping,
and overhead, Yasmin, the locally dis-
assembled, the wingèd, pointing down and proudly beaming.

Upon such sacrifices the gods themselves shy clods.

Riffling the pages of sorrow and suffering,
the President carefully lowers his hydroce-
     phalic head onto the news he made.

Besides, the State abhors the inner life, finds
     its rich wantlessness, its invisible rev-
     erie uninteresting because unmanageable,
     damned because unusable. Incapable
     of inactivity, the State cannot submit to
     stillness and seeks precisely to create the
     desire it will manage. It requires neither
     pensive persons nor upright citizens but
     a smiling multitude. The State is a Midas.
     Every absence and invisibility it would
     make bright material, for what is invisi-
     ble—Deif's resolve to return the money
     or patient grief recollecting the spilt
     petals of his lost jasmine—what is invisi-
     ble the State believes deplorable, knows
     to be dangerous. Such is the anxiety that
     caused the President to lift a finger, to
     touch Deif.

To reconstitute the found Fiat as the lost
     daughter.

Wheeled, powerful, in progress; altar and throne
and golden veal, leviathan and juggernaut;
and nearby, one Reda Deif—once slowly
exploding, once a spirit darkening
all earthly glory—observes the State
adoring itself as its image.

Deif attending the vehicle.
His *air de chauffeur*, a man
who defers to a car, infers
his value from his deference.
He bows, approaching the door,

bows to the aura and glory
around, behind, beyond, within
this scrap of State, this scrim
of status before the reeling stars;
he bows to be bowing. Air
now of one waiting for
its owner to appear. Deif knows
it can't be Deif, must be another:
grand, glowing, ponderous, a meteor,
breathtaker and heartstealer, mover and shaker,
who merely presuming possesses,
imposes, distresses between his flashing
attraction, his haughty don't-touch!
Let poorman-Deif dare show his face,
guarddog-Deif will show him the door!
He shifts from foot to foot
beside himself beside the car.
Embarrassment? Well,
ecstasy.

Seepage of eternity we call the sea, the sky.
Such spacious summer nights come also to Deif,
the sky enormous, intimate, Deif too brief, too dusky.
The universe invites him to fly—if only he *could* fly!
It snatches his heart and throws it into the blue,
the cosmic wafting blows it away.
Must I? Must I follow?
he asks the whirlwind's roar.
His heart will shatter to encompass all
or, lightless coal, plummet through the dark and azure!
Lies down again, throbbing, where he was. Schlemiel
and saint and monster are cradled and tucked in.

However theatrically laid on thick by fate, how did this tiny
   whisper of injustice exceed the general and deafening
   static of woe?
Do you think Deif's boss called a press conference to announce
   the shafting?

Or that his neighbors issued a news release?
Do you think Deif himself told the story?
Really? him? that schlemiel? And to whom in that Calcutta
    on the Nile?
Maybe you think it doesn't flatter the President a little too
    neatly?
Think it isn't the least bit imaginary?
No poets of Presidency in Egypt?
No P.R. men in Cairo?
Do you think there really is a man named Deif?

I think I prefer to think that Deif exists,
yes, and even little Yasmin dead dead dead
indeed, dead for a fact.
I think I prefer this horror
which tells me it is possible to feel
if not to believe.
Only horror survives our raging irony
and we survive by horror.

So one delves a death and turns ... a pretty penny,
some moral quid for all that mortal quo (O wit
for woe!)—O "think" and "feel," increments
of spirit that transfuse, that elevate! Tumescent
atop her grave, and how a great heart gushes, floods
the frame with gladdening news: One *has* come through!
—which makes one, after all, complicit, one's spade
a spade, Yasmin, Deif one's victims, one's life
vicarious, vacant, oneself a fiction
held up to a fate, shattered by a fury.
Pluck out your radio, rend your paper!
Savage death demands a savage discipline.
Down your head, roll in the dirt, mourn!

As to bad before, so now to better fortune:
Deif submits. Incorrigible schlemiel,
he doesn't grab it with both hands,
one on each tit. See him!

insulated from the earth by rubber,
two fingers gingerly on the wheel,
his other arm out to catch the breeze
as he drives into the sunset of the real,
his position false but increasingly familiar.
Fortune sits on him like a ton of shit
—a raven of another choler—and smiles.
Sociably, he returns the smile.

Farewell, Deif! Farewell, brother!

Impatient to be under way, he boarded early; still the boat delayed at quayside, then floated off into the house of spooks. What a disappointment that was! Where are the real terrors, he demanded, for which he'd spent his life preparing? Oh, but the eulogy of terror—*any* eulogy—would have stultified his dying, kept him as he was, an aging man becalmed in the luminous still sea of his transcendence. Instead, these too obvious frights, all burlap and cotton batting and sprung wires, an old mattress dump, unbelievable!—it wouldn't fool, much less terrify, a child—and revolting! the stink swaddled his head, he would have vomited—and then the wine- and urine-stewed supers who manned its machinery, headsmen and skeletons, murderous crones and farting trumps that made a pass at troubling the dark—couldn't the universe do any better than that! What a sendoff, who'd *want* to come back! So he kibitzed his dying, feeling mocked and cheated, it was so unworthy, so demeaning.

Of course, something kibitzed him back. That was the ordeal of laughter. (It could have been better.) Storms of hooting and heckling drove him backward, each affronting buffet pushily took a bit of his life. Swept away, unable not to be where he'd been before, how much he should have liked to join in the party, draw power from the chorus of wise guys and with it howl out the last laugh, be *named* Laughter—mockery's own mascot— and claw his way back to himself, to anywhere! But the laugh machine really *was* laughing— to itself and yet at him, as if it were his own râling breath, mocking and sustaining, or this little boat of wires and tubes that bore him so poorly. Mad, mechanical, unreal, still the laughter was appropriate and, therefore, genuine, had to possess *some* understanding. He saw that. He *was* ridiculous, not heroic at all, a little boy, and maybe less than that, a baby, probably, who couldn't wipe his own behind. And all his rage a huffing grotesquerie, as if to give death a scare—it was right to boot him out of the world like this. Absurd to be so helpless! Ridiculous to be so absurd! Nevertheless, the ritual of derision did not fail him, secured his passage and kept him company all the way.

Even in the first instant of its fiat, the
voice of God seemed badly dubbed, the words
a curb in the mouth that outran sound. Never-
theless, at the end of time as at its beginning,
cracked, clouded, flickering, thin, the light
that responded touched everything with its
original clarity, its first glory.

In memory of Lionel Trilling

The age's principled ingratitude,
a viscous cant of self-begetting,
as if we *realized, fulfilled* a *self,*
who are indeed fictive and empty,
transparencies where eyebeams cross:
the points of intersection blaze
into sight, a sudden glory, light
looks back at light, star sees star,
and together are the shining of heaven.
And now and now and now an eye blinks off.
Unseen, I feel invisible, destroyed.
And every eye will shut away the luster,
and we and all will be again
the volatile nothing, and clear clear dark.

This major new collection of poems
re-establishes Irving Feldman as "one of
the most engaging and powerful poets
of his generation," as Lionel Trilling
described him in 1972. Several impor-
tant new poems—not only "Leaping
Clear" but "Beethoven's Bust" and
"The Golden Schlemiel"—are found
here, along with new and unexpected
treasures that demonstrate Mr. Feld-
man's remarkable depth and range.
These are poems of great clarity; the
voice is at once passionate and lyrical,
the tone both spare and deeply reso-
nant. "This is the real thing," as a critic
wrote of Mr. Feldman's earlier work,
"honest, hard-bought, and a tonic ex-
perience for anyone who may have
doubted the plausibility of coming up-
on something rich, strange and new."